THIS BOOK BELONGS TO

.........Thea................

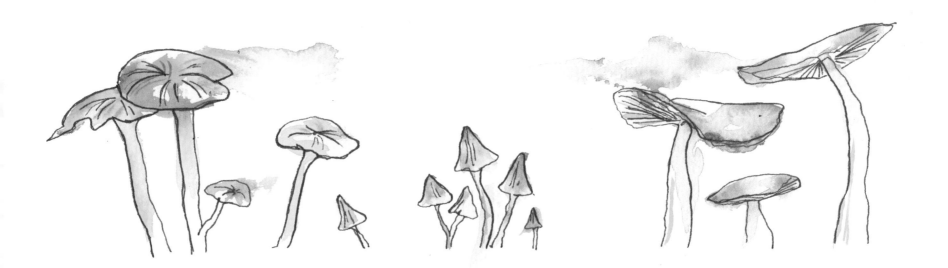

ISBN 978–1–9164746–0–4

There was once a young red squirrel called Sandy who lived with his family in a Scottish pinewood near Inverness. Every morning the family woke up at first light and headed out into the woods to search for food.

Most of the time they ate the seeds from pinecones, but they also nibbled on lichen growing on trees, on flowers and berries and, in the autumn, hazelnuts and acorns.

Sandy's favourite food of all was mushrooms, and he thought the tastiest way to eat them was after his mother had hung them out on tree branches to dry.

At night he curled up in a drey built high in a tree with his mother and two sisters. The drey was woven tightly out of sticks and was lined with moss and leaves to keep the family warm and cosy, but, now that Sandy and his sisters were nearly grown up, it was getting a bit small for them all.

His mother had recently started saying that the young squirrels would need to leave home soon and find a new forest to live in where they would have to build dreys of their own.

Sandy didn't like this idea very much – he felt safe and secure with his family and found the thought of leaving pretty scary.

In a big oak tree nearby lived Sandy's best friend, Rusty, and his family. They slept in an old hole in the tree trunk, which they had made into a cosy nest.

Sandy and Rusty were the same age, and every day they played their favourite games of chasing each other through the branches and hiding nuts to see if the other one could find them. But, whereas Sandy preferred to stay close to home, Rusty was very adventurous and always wanted to go off exploring.

"Oh, come on Sandy. Stop being so boring – we might find loads of tasty mushrooms if we go a little bit further away!"

5

Rusty's mother had also told him that soon the time would come for him to leave home, but, unlike Sandy, he was very excited by this thought and couldn't wait to head off and find the perfect wood in which to settle down.

One morning, when Rusty woke up, his mother called him to her and said that they needed to have a very important talk. "Now Rusty, I know in a few weeks' time you'll be ready to leave home and find a new wood of your own to live in, so I need to tell you about some of the dangers of the wider world."

"Oh Mum, I've heard it all a thousand times. I know I need to watch out for pine martens and buzzards, and a pine marten would never catch me anyway – I'm far too fast!"

"Well, I'm glad to hear you've paid attention to what I've said, Rusty, although your great uncle Sciurus was nearly caught by a pine marten once. He just escaped but lost the end of his tail, so don't be too cocky! But I need to tell you about something much more dangerous than that, so please listen carefully."

"Okay", groaned Rusty and settled himself down to see what on earth could be so scary.

"Rusty," began his mother, "the greatest threat to us red squirrels is not pine martens or buzzards – it's grey squirrels."

"Grey squirrels?" asked Rusty. "Aren't all squirrels red?"

"No", replied his mother. "Long ago every squirrel that lived in Britain was red, but then humans brought some grey squirrels over from America and released them into the woods in England. They didn't think the grey squirrels would do any harm, but Rusty – they've been killing us red squirrels ever since!"

"But how?" asked Rusty. "Do they attack us?"

"No", said his mother. "The problem is that they eat all our food before we can; they are bigger and can eat acorns and other foods before they're ripe, which leaves nothing left for us reds. And they also dig up the food supplies that we bury to see us through winter and eat those. Rusty, grey squirrels have spread all through England and Wales, and they've wiped us reds out wherever they've gone!"

"You mean there aren't any red squirrels left in England or Wales?" asked Rusty. "Only a few", sighed his mother.

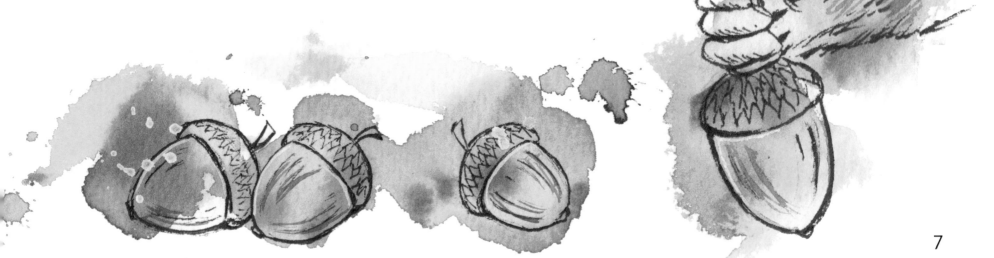

Rusty felt very glad that he didn't live anywhere near England or Wales but couldn't understand why his mother was so worried. "But we're ok up here in Scotland, aren't we Mum? I've never seen a grey squirrel in these woods." "Oh Rusty", said his mother wearily. "We're very lucky that there aren't any grey squirrels just where we live, but they are in Scotland and not far away, so that's why I wanted to speak to you about it because you'll be leaving home soon. I know you're a very adventurous young squirrel, and you'll probably want to travel a long way, but you MUST NOT head south or east because that's where the grey squirrels are."

Rusty's mother could see that what she had said had unnerved him a little. He didn't normally worry about anything, and so she said "Anyway, I know you won't be leaving for a while yet, and, as long as you don't travel too far away from here, you should be fine. Now, why don't you go and find Sandy and have a good game before lunch? I've got some mushrooms that are just about ready for eating, and, if you're lucky, I might dig out

a few hazelnuts that I've got stored away from last autumn as well."

Rusty headed off outside, but he didn't go to find Sandy straight away. The news his mother had given him had scared him a little, and he wanted to find out more about grey squirrels and how they might affect his plans to go off on a big adventure. He knew who would be a good squirrel to talk to – wise old Mr. Whiskers, who lived on the edge of their wood in the branches of a big oak tree.

He set off for Mr. Whiskers', stopping to feed on a few pine cones as he went. When he arrived, the old squirrel greeted him and offered him some freshly picked oak flowers to nibble on.

"Now, what brings you here, young Master Rusty?" he enquired. "Hi Mr. Whiskers. I wanted to ask your advice about grey squirrels; my Mum has just been telling me all about them because I'll be leaving home soon, so I wanted to find out as much as I can."

"Oh blimey, Rusty. That's a very serious matter to be talking about on a lovely sunny day like this, but it's best that you know all about the dangers, so come on in."

Once they were settled inside, Mr. Whiskers began. "Now, I suppose your mother has told you all about how they take our food and cause us to starve, but did she mention the horrible disease that they carry?" "No – no – she didn't" gasped Rusty. "What disease is that?" "Well, it's called Squirrel pox, Rusty. It doesn't harm the grey squirrels or humans, but it kills us reds, so it's very, very dangerous for us to go anywhere near a grey squirrel."

Mr. Whiskers then carried on talking about other things like the noisy badgers that lived under the roots of his oak tree, but Rusty wasn't really listening any more. For the first time in his life he felt worried about his future; where was he to go and what would happen if he did meet a grey squirrel?

Over the next few days Rusty and Sandy continued to play their usual games together, but Rusty's mind was on other things. His mother had said that grey squirrels were living not very far away, and he wanted to get as far away from them as he could. He decided it was time to tell Sandy about the dangers

and to persuade him to leave home with him as soon as possible.

The next morning Rusty broke the news to his friend. Sandy's eyes widened as he learned about the thousands of red squirrels that had starved because of the greys and about the dreadful disease called Squirrel pox. "Sandy, we need to leave now and head either north or west to get as far away from them as possible!" urged Rusty. But Sandy shook his head. "Rusty, haven't you heard? We can't go very far either north or west because people have cut all the trees down and there isn't any forest left for us there." "Oh, nuts!" exclaimed Rusty. "Those humans have really caused us lots of problems, haven't they? But never mind. We might not be able to get all the way, but we should certainly go as far as we can; the further away from the greys we can get, the better. Let's leave tomorrow!"

Sandy didn't like the sound of leaving so early; he'd been looking forward to another few weeks at home with his mother and sisters, but he had to admit that they'd have to leave soon anyway, and going with his friend Rusty certainly seemed like a much better idea than heading off by himself.

The next morning the two young squirrels said goodbye to their families. "Now, you be careful out there", warned their mothers tearfully as they hugged them. "Watch out for pine martens, keep an eye overhead for buzzards, stay away from humans and, most important of all, don't go anywhere near a grey squirrel!"

Sandy and Rusty set off through the forest They decided to head for a wooded hill on the horizon, which was further than either of them had ever travelled before.

It took much longer to get there than they had imagined, and, by the time they arrived, it was starting to get dark and they were both exhausted and very hungry. "Tell you what", said Rusty. "I'll find us a nice hole in a tree to sleep in tonight, and you have a scout around and find us some tasty pine cones."

Whilst Sandy headed into the canopy to search for food, Rusty scampered down onto the forest floor to look for a suitable tree. Suddenly, from out of nowhere, a dark, menacing shape loomed up in front of him and, although he'd never seen a pine marten before, he knew immediately from his mother's description what it was. It leaped straight at him! "Eeeek!" shrieked Rusty – "Help!" He raced away over the forest floor as fast as he could with the pine marten hot on his heels. He dodged this way and that, but the pine marten was getting closer and closer and, when he turned his head, he saw its long claws stretched out ready to grab him!

Just in time, Rusty jumped up into the nearest tree, thinking he'd be safe there. But the pine marten followed him up! Rusty dodged round and round the tree and then scampered out onto a branch, but the pine marten kept coming – he could feel its hot breath on his back!

Just as it was about to lunge at him, Rusty took a massive leap and somehow managed to land in the next tree. Luckily, the branch wasn't strong enough to hold the pine marten's weight, and so it stopped in the first tree and didn't follow. "Oh, thank goodness!" panted Rusty as he stopped to catch his breath. "Mum was right – now I understand what happened to poor Uncle Sciurus!"

In the meantime, Sandy had made a discovery. He had hopped between a few trees, looking for some tasty pine cones, when, suddenly, he had smelled something he didn't recognise. He had followed his nose and had come to a strange looking object attached to a tree. It was a sort of wire cage, although Sandy didn't realise it was a cage, never having seen such a thing before, and inside were some nuts in a pot. The nuts had smelled absolutely delicious, and so he had hopped inside and eaten some.

After feasting for a few minutes, he called out to Rusty to come to join him but got no reply. He kept calling, but still Rusty didn't come, and by now it was dark. "Oh no", thought Sandy sadly. "Where on earth is Rusty?"

After a final few shouts Sandy realised that his friend wasn't going to come back and that he was going to have to spend the night by himself, all alone, in a strange wood. He didn't have a drey to sleep in or even a cosy nest hole where he'd be safe from predators. The only thing he could do was to sleep on a branch and hope that he'd be alright until morning, so he wrapped his tail around his head and curled up as tightly as he could.

Thankfully, although he spent most of the night shivering and having nightmares about marauding pine martens and buzzards, he woke up at first light still in one piece.

"I'll have a good search around and see if I can find Rusty", he thought. "Then I'll have some breakfast."

He shouted and shouted and searched and searched for Rusty but could find no sign of his friend. Feeling very sad and alone, he scampered along to the tree where he'd found the nuts the night before.

Strangely, the pot was full again! "Oh how wonderful!" thought Sandy. "At least I have some food."

He hopped inside the cage, but, just as he reached the nuts, the door of the cage swung shut with a massive crash. He was trapped! "Ahhhhhh", screamed Sandy. "I can't get out!" Desperately, he pushed and pulled but could not open the door or find any other way out,

and then, to make matters even worse, he saw a human approaching! He suddenly began to get really scared, especially when he saw that the human had a pair of scissors in her hand – was she going to cut off his bushy red tail?

The person came right up to the cage and cut it down from the tree, with Sandy frantically charging around inside, trying to get out. She set it down on the ground and covered it over with a dark cloth, but what Sandy heard next came as a real surprise. "Don't worry – I'm not going to hurt you", said the lady.

When Sandy heard the kindly tone in her voice, he felt a little better and a bit calmer now that he was in darkness. The lady carried the cage to a car, talking softly all the while to Sandy. "It's okay little squirrel – I'm going to take you to the west coast of Scotland. It's a long way from here, but there are no grey squirrels there, so you'll be safe."

Sandy couldn't believe what the lady had just said. He had heard his grandparents talk about the old forests of the west coast; they had told him wondrous tales of hazel, oak and pine woods stretching for miles. However, they had also told him that, although red squirrels used to live in the west, they had died out long ago because humans had cut down much of the forest. He wondered what on earth was going to happen to him; he would apparently be safe from grey squirrels, but it sounded like he would have to fend for himself on open ground with no trees, and he would be all by himself – his grandparents had said there hadn't been any red squirrels in the west for at least 50 years!

At that moment the lady started the car, and all thoughts went out of Sandy's mind as he listened in terror to the roar of the engine and felt the vibrations rumble all through his body.

After what seemed like an age, the car stopped. "Thank goodness", thought Sandy.

But his ordeal didn't end there. The next thing he knew, he was being taken out of the cage and was being weighed and measured. "Don't worry little squirrel. I'm sorry to scare you, but you'll be ok soon. I'm just checking that you're fit and healthy, so that I can take you across to the west coast", said the lady.

At last the lady let go of Sandy and placed him gently into a box. It was lined with hay and had some food in. "Phew!" thought Sandy – "It seems safer in here, and there are some of those yummy nuts and some apple as well." He hadn't realised it, but, after all the effort of trying to get out of the cage, he was parched, and the apple would be just the thing to quench his thirst.

After a few more hours of driving, which seemed like a lifetime to Sandy, the car stopped again, and he was picked up in his box and carried for a while. As he was shut in the dark, he didn't know what was going on, but he felt the box being lifted up high and heard a few human voices and a drilling sound as the box was secured to a tree, that was almost as terrifying as the car engine. Then all went quiet.

He lay trembling in the box for a few minutes, wondering what on earth was going to happen to him next.

After a while he noticed there was a chink of light shining into the box and then realised

that there was a hole there – a hole that looked big enough for him to get out of! There was some moss blocking his way, but he thought he could push through that easily enough. After lying still for a good while longer to be sure that there were no humans about, he decided to go for it. He took a flying jump at the hole, and, sure enough, the moss fell straight out!

19

Perching on the edge of the hole, looking out of the box, a whole new world met his eyes. There was forest stretching as far as he could see, and, beyond that, something blue was glistening – the sea! "Wow", he exclaimed. "So this is the west coast!"

Sandy continued to stare in amazement for a few minutes and then ventured out of the box. He set off down the tree to investigate his new surroundings, his mind in a whirl. "Things could be a lot worse. The humans haven't harmed me; they've brought me to the west, and it looks like a wonderful place for a red squirrel. My grandparents must have got it wrong about it all being cut down, but there aren't any other squirrels here, and being all by myself forever won't be much fun!"

He jumped down onto the forest floor and set off to have a closer look at the sea, which he had never seen before, and then he suddenly heard a shout. "Sandy! Sandy! Is that you?" He spun around to see another squirrel racing towards him. "Rusty? No way – you're here too!" Sandy exclaimed.

Suddenly a great wave of relief surged through him – if his best friend was here as well, then surely everything would be alright after all.

The two squirrels chattered away to each other non-stop with Rusty trying to tell Sandy all about the pine marten that had chased him and Sandy re-living the horrors of the cage and everything that had happened afterwards.

Eventually, Rusty interrupted him. "Sandy, exactly the same thing happened to me, but I think I can explain a bit more about it. There were two humans in the car that brought me over here, and I could hear them talking. They have a plan to bring lots of red squirrels to the west coast of Scotland; apparently the forest used to be very widespread here until humans cut it down, but since then they've planted more trees, and it's now perfect for us red squirrels! We couldn't have got here by ourselves because there is still a lot of open ground without trees in between here and where our families are. But Sandy, guess what the best bit of all is – there are no grey squirrels here! The humans were saying that what they're doing is really important because we will be protected from grey squirrels as they can't cross the open ground either. Sandy, we're safe – they've rescued us!"

Suddenly, the two squirrels started laughing. They had both had a terrible fright, but their ordeals were over now, and they knew that they were safe – safer than they had ever been before. They set off to explore their new forest together, marvelling at the heavy clusters of hazelnuts and acorns on the trees, but they both knew exactly what it was that they needed to celebrate their new-found freedom. "Come on Sandy', said Rusty happily. "I think it's time to find some mushrooms!"

FUN FACTS ABOUT RED SQUIRRELS

Red squirrels have a very varied diet – they eat pine cones, flowers, buds, berries, fungi, bird eggs, insects, lichen and much more.

Red squirrels chew on discarded deer antlers and bones to get calcium!

Red squirrels do not hibernate. They spend the autumn months burying nuts and other food underground and hiding them in crevices in trees. This provides them with food for the winter.

A red squirrel can tell if a nut is good or not by holding it in its paws!

In wintertime, red squirrels have ear tufts, but these normally disappear in summer when they moult.

Just like humans, red squirrels can be either left- or right-handed, or pawed!

Baby red squirrels are called kittens. The average litter size is 3–4 but can be as many as 6. They are born in a cosy drey – a ball of sticks lined with grasses, moss and hair for warmth, built high in a tree.

Red squirrels really do hang mushrooms out to dry on tree branches!

A REAL-LIFE STORY

This book is based on the Red Squirrel Reintroduction Project which is being carried out by the charity Trees for Life. So far, more than 140 red squirrels have been caught from areas where they are numerous and have been relocated to the northwest Scottish Highlands. The new populations are free from grey squirrels, and they are flourishing and helping to increase the numbers of red squirrels in the UK.

10% of the proceeds from this book is being donated to Trees for Life to help safeguard red squirrels for the future.

Visit treesforlife.org.uk to learn more.

Lightning Source UK Ltd.
Milton Keynes UK
UKRC011003290620
365745UK00001B/3